This book belongs to . . .

_____

D1470751

www.makebelieveideas.co.uk

Written by Rosie Greening.
Illustrated by Clare Fennell.

TEN little CHICKS

Clare Fennell · Rosie Greening

make
believe
ideas

10 little, fluffy **CHiCKS** are hatching in a line.

One gets **stuck** inside her **egg**, so that leaves . . .

9 little, speedy CHiCKS are learning how to skate.

One can't work out how to **stop**, so that leaves . . .

8 little, chirping **CHiCKS** relax in **picnic** heaven.

One wants to make daisy chains, so that leaves . . .

7 little, funny CHICKS
are doing circus tricks.

One **drops** all his juggling balls, so that leaves . . .

6 little, splashing CHICKS
are taking turns to dive.

One decides to **chicken out,** so that leaves . . .

5 little, friendly **CHICKS**
hear a loud . . . .

"Hee-haw!"

One goes for a
donkey ride,
so that leaves . . .

4 little, laughing CH!CKS go through a maze with glee.

One gets **lost** in all the **corn**, so that leaves . . .

3 little, helpful **CHICKS** have lots of **chores** to do.

One soon needs to **wash** his wings, so that leaves . . .

2 little, racing **CHICKS** are having lots of fun.

One comes last and starts to **sulk**, so that leaves . . .

1 little, lonely **CHICK** would like to celebrate.

But all her friends have **disappeared**,
and now it's getting **late!**

10 little, happy **CHiCKS** wear **costumes** that they've made.

Their **friends** are here – it's time to **cheer**
and have a big **parade!**